Jack, be nimble,
Jack, be quick,
Jack, jump over
The candlestick.

Richard
Scarry's

Best
MOTHER
GOOSE
Ever

Ring a ring o' roses,
A pocket full of posies,
A-tishoo! A-tishoo!
We all fall down.

A GOLDEN BOOK • NEW YORK

Golden Books Publishing Company, Inc., New York, New York 10106

6

Index of First Lines

Little Boy Blue,
   Come blow your horn!
The sheep's in the meadow,
   The cow's in the corn.

Where is the little boy
   Tending the sheep?
He's under the haycock,
   Fast asleep.

Will you wake him?
   No, not I;
For if I do,
   He's sure to cry.

When I was a bachelor I lived by myself,
And all the bread and cheese I got I laid up on the shelf;
The rats and the mice, they made such a strife,
I had to go to London to buy me a wife.

The streets were so bad and the lanes were so narrow,
I was forced to bring my wife home in a wheelbarrow.
The wheelbarrow broke and my wife had a fall;
Down came wheelbarrow, little wife and all.

Bobby Shafto's gone to sea,
  Silver buckles at his knee;
He'll come back and marry me,
  Bonny Bobby Shafto!

Bobby Shafto's fat and fair,
  Combing down his yellow hair;
He's my love for evermore,
  Bonny Bobby Shafto!

Tom, Tom, the piper's son,
Stole a pig and away did run.
The pig was eat, and Tom was beat,
And Tom went crying down the street.

London Bridge is falling down,
  Falling down, falling down.
London Bridge is falling down,
  My fair lady.

Build it up with wood and clay,
  Wood and clay, wood and clay,
Build it up with wood and clay,
  My fair lady.

One misty, moisty morning,
When cloudy was the weather,
I chanced to meet an old man
Clothed all in leather.
Clothed all in leather,
With cap under his chin.
How do you do, and how do you do,
And how do you do again?

19

There was an old woman who lived in a shoe.
She had so many children she didn't know what
   to do.
She gave them some broth without any bread,
   scolded them soundly and sent them to bed.

20

Simple Simon met a pieman,
    Going to the fair;
Says Simple Simon to the pieman,
    Let me taste your ware.

Says the pieman to Simple Simon,
    Show me first your penny;
Says Simple Simon to the pieman,
    Indeed, I have not any.

Hickety, pickety, my fine hen,
She lays eggs for gentlemen;
Gentlemen come every day
To see what my fine hen doth lay.
Sometimes nine and sometimes ten,
Hickety, pickety, my fine hen.

Diddle, diddle, dumpling, my son John,
Went to bed with his trousers on;
One shoe off, and one shoe on;
Diddle, diddle, dumpling, my son John.

I do not like thee, Doctor Fell,
The reason why I cannot tell;
But this I know, and know full well,
I do not like thee, Doctor Fell.

27

There were once two cats of Kilkenny,
Each thought there was one cat too many;
So they fought and they fit,
And they scratched and they bit,
Till, excepting their nails
And the tips of their tails,
Instead of two cats, there weren't any.

Georgie Porgie, pudding and pie,
Kissed the girls and made them cry;
When the boys came out to play,
Georgie Porgie ran away.

Hey diddle, diddle,
The cat and the fiddle,
The cow jumped over the moon;
The little dog laughed
To see such sport,
And the dish ran away with the spoon.

Old Mother Hubbard
Went to the cupboard
To fetch her poor dog a bone;
But when she got there
The cupboard was bare,
And so the poor dog had none.

She went to the grocer's
To buy him some fruit;
But when she came back
He was playing the flute.

She went to the hatter's
To buy him a hat;
But when she came back
He was feeding the cat.

34

She went to the tailor's
To buy him a coat;
But when she came back
He was riding a goat.

The dame made a curtsey,
The dog made a bow;
The dame said, Your servant,
The dog said, Bow-wow.

35

Baa, baa, black sheep,
Have you any wool?
Yes, sir, yes, sir,
Three bags full;
One for my master,
One for my dame,
And one for the little boy
Who lives down the lane.

Polly, put the kettle on,
Polly, put the kettle on,
Polly, put the kettle on,
   We'll all have tea.

Sukey, take it off again,
Sukey, take it off again,
Sukey, take it off again,
   They've all gone away.

Elsie Marley is grown so fine,
She won't get up to feed the swine,
But lies in bed till eight or nine,
Lazy Elsie Marley.

Old Mother Goose,
When she wanted to wander,
Would ride through the air
On a very fine gander.

42

Rub-a-dub-dub,
Three men in a tub;
And who do you think they be?
The butcher, the baker,
The candlestick-maker;
Turn 'em out, knaves all three!

43

To market, to market, to buy a fat pig,
Home again, home again, jiggety-jig;
To market, to market, to buy a fat hog,
Home again, home again, jiggety-jog.

Peter, Peter, pumpkin eater,
Had a wife and couldn't keep her;
He put her in a pumpkin shell
And there he kept her very well.

Sing a song of sixpence,
  A pocket full of rye;
Four and twenty blackbirds
  Baked in a pie!

When the pie was opened,
  The birds began to sing;
Wasn't that a dainty dish
  To set before the king?

The king was in his counting-house,
  Counting out his money;
The queen was in the parlor,
  Eating bread and honey.

The maid was in the garden,
  Hanging out the clothes;
There came a little blackbird,
  And snipped off her nose!

Barber, barber, shave a pig,
How many hairs to make a wig?
Four and twenty, that's enough.
Give the barber a pinch of snuff.

50

Peter Piper picked a peck of pickled peppers;
A peck of pickled peppers Peter Piper picked.
If Peter Piper picked a peck of pickled peppers,
Where's the peck of pickled peppers Peter Piper picked?

Jack Sprat could eat no fat,
His wife could eat no lean,
And so between them both, you see,
They licked the platter clean.

There was a jolly miller once,
  Lived on the river Dee;
He worked and sang from morn till night,
  No lark more blithe than he.

And this the burden of his song
  Forever used to be—
I care for nobody, no! not I,
  If nobody cares for me.

Old King Cole
Was a merry old soul,
And a merry old soul was he;
He called for his pipe,
And he called for his bowl,
And he called for his fiddlers three.

Every fiddler, he had a fine fiddle,
And a very fine fiddle had he;
Twee tweedle dee, tweedle dee, went the fiddlers.
Oh, there's none so rare
As can compare
With King Cole and his fiddlers three.

Fe, fi, fo, fum,
I smell the blood of an Englishman;
Be he alive or be he dead,
I'll grind his bones to make my bread.

Three little kittens,
They lost their mittens,
And they began to cry,
Oh, mother dear, we sadly fear
Our mittens we have lost.

What! Lost your mittens,
You naughty kittens!
Then you shall have no pie.
Mee-ow, mee-ow, mee-ow.
No, you shall have no pie.

The three little kittens,
They found their mittens,
And they began to cry,
Oh, mother dear, see here, see here,
Our mittens we have found.

What! Found your mittens,
You silly kittens!
Then you shall have some pie.
Purr-r, purr-r, purr-r,
Oh, let us have some pie.

The three little kittens,
Put on their mittens,
And soon ate up the pie;
Oh, mother dear, we greatly fear
Our mittens we have soiled.

What! Soiled your mittens,
You naughty kittens!
Then they began to sigh,
Mee-ow, mee-ow, mee-ow.
Then they began to sigh.

The three little kittens,
They washed their mittens,
And hung them out to dry;
Oh, mother dear, look here, look here,
Our mittens we have washed.

What! Washed your mittens?
You're good little kittens.
But I smell a rat close by!
Hush! Hush! Hush!
I smell a rat close by.

The cat sat asleep by the side of the fire,
The mistress snored loud as a pig;
Jack took up his fiddle by Jenny's desire,
And struck up a bit of a jig.

Little maid, pretty maid, whither goest thou?
Down in the meadow to milk my cow.
Shall I go with thee? No, not now;
When I send for thee, then come thou.

One, two,
Buckle my shoe;

Three, four,
Knock at the door;

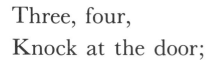

Five, six,
Pick up sticks;

Seven, eight,
Lay them straight;

Nine, ten,
A big fat hen.

A dillar, a dollar,
A ten-o'clock scholar,
What makes you come so soon?
You used to come at ten o'clock,
And now you come at noon.

69

Pussy cat, pussy cat, where have you been?
I've been to London to look at the queen.
Pussy cat, pussy cat, what did you there?
I frightened a little mouse under her chair.

Hector Protector was dressed all in green;
Hector Protector was sent to the queen.
The queen did not like him,
No more did the king;
So Hector Protector was sent back again.

Taffy was a Welshman,
  Taffy was a thief,
Taffy came to my house
  And stole a piece of beef.

I went to Taffy's house,
  Taffy wasn't in,
I jumped upon his Sunday hat
  And poked it with a pin.

Taffy was a Welshman,
  Taffy was a sham,
Taffy came to my house
  And stole a leg of lamb.

I went to Taffy's house,
   Taffy was away,
I stuffed his socks with sawdust
   And filled his shoes with clay.

Taffy was a Welshman,
   Taffy was a cheat,
Taffy came to my house
   And stole a piece of meat.

I went to Taffy's house,
   Taffy was in bed,
I took a marrow bone
   And beat him on the head.

Mistress Mary, quite contrary,
How does your garden grow?
With silver bells and cockle shells,
And pretty maids all in a row.

Little Miss Muffet
Sat on a tuffet,
Eating her curds and whey;
There came a big spider,
Who sat down beside her,
And frightened Miss Muffet away.

I had a little hen,
    The prettiest ever seen;
She washed up the dishes,
    And kept the house clean;
She went to the mill
    To fetch me some flour,
And always got home
    In less than an hour;

She baked me my bread,
    She brewed me my ale;
She sat by the fire
    And told a fine tale.

79

Blow, wind, blow! and go, mill, go!
That the miller may grind his corn;
  That the baker may take it,
  And into bread make it,
And bring us a loaf in the morn.

As I was going to St. Ives,
I met a man with seven wives.
Every wife had seven sacks,
Every sack had seven cats,
Every cat had seven kits;
Kits, cats, sacks and wives,
How many were going to St. Ives?

This little pig went to market,

This little pig stayed home,

This little pig had roast beef,   This little pig had none,

And this little pig cried, Wee-wee-wee-wee-wee,

I can't find my way home.

Pussy cat, pussy cat,
    Wilt thou be mine?
Thou shalt not wash dishes
    Nor yet feed the swine,
But sit on a cushion
    And sew a fine seam
And feed upon strawberries,
    Sugar and cream.

Wee Willie Winkie runs through the town,
Upstairs and downstairs, in his nightgown;
Rapping at the window, crying through the lock,
Are the children all in bed, for now it's eight o'clock?

Star light, star bright,
First star I see tonight,
I wish I may, I wish I might,
Have the wish I wish tonight.

Good night,
Sleep tight,
Wake up bright
In the morning light,
To do what's right
With all your might.

There was an old crow
    Sat upon a clod;
That's the end of my song.
    ——That's odd.